MARIELLA QUEEN OF THE SKIES

EOIN COLFER

WITH ILLUSTRATIONS BY
KATY HALFORD

Barrington Stoke

First published in 2018 in Great Britain by
Barrington Stoke Ltd
18 Walker Street, Edinburgh, EH3 7LP

www.barringtonstoke.co.uk

A CIP catalogue record for this book is available from the British Library upon request

ISBN: 978-1-78112-770-4

Printed in China by Leo

This book is in a super readable format for young readers beginning their independent reading journey.

CONTENTS

1 Right and Wrong 1

2 Spinning Tops and Bananas 9

3 Day and Night 19

4 Anti-Matter Rays and Holes in the Fabric of Time 27

5 Cannons and Catapults (and mashed apple too) 35

6 Spiders and Stars 43

7 Three Days and Three Nights 55

8 Jumping Jacks and Snakeskins 67

9 New Friends and Lollipops 79

CHAPTER 1

Right and Wrong

There was once a girl called Mariella who was super smart and spent her days inventing. Mariella's head was always bursting with ideas. But she was only happy when she could turn her ideas into real things.

Most of the time Mariella thought that her ideas were great.

Two examples of this were her robot SURPRISE BALL! which kept her baby brother Harrison busy for hours, and then the Jump Rope Twizzler, which was very handy if a girl only had one friend to do skipping with.

But sometimes things did go wrong.

One example of this was the toilet seat sensor, which Mariella invented to stop Buster drinking from the bowl. Mariella didn't like to talk about that one.

CHAPTER 2

Spinning Tops and Bananas

'There are not enough hours in the day for all my inventing ideas,' Mariella thought.

As soon as the sun set, it was off to bed for Mariella and no arguments. And bedtime always seemed to arrive at the wrong moment.

One evening Mum came down to the lab when Mariella was really busy and not in the mood for interruptions.

"Bedtime, sweetie," Mum said. "And I don't want to hear that you're inventing."

“Ten more minutes, Mum, please,” Mariella pleaded. “I AM inventing. Right now I’m working on a spinning top with fifteen blades that could change for ever the way we peel bananas.”

Mum was not impressed. “That sounds dangerous, Mariella,” she said. “And we already have inventions for peeling bananas. They are called fingers.”

Mariella knew that there was no point in arguing with Mum.

She shut down her equipment and tramped upstairs. She had one cup of hot chocolate and two stories, and then she slid down under her duvet – the one with a picture of the Periodic Table on it.

The last thought Mariella had before she dropped off to sleep was – 'Bedtime. No more!'

CHAPTER 3

Day and Night

Mariella woke up thinking the exact same thing – 'Bedtime. No more!'

Mariella put her big brain to work to solve the Problem of Bedtime and spent all that weekend trying to invent something that would get her out of going to bed.

First of all, she built a fake Mariella to take her place.

But Buster the dog wasn't fooled for an instant.

Then she put up sun lamps outside all the windows so her parents would think it was still daytime even when it was bedtime.

But, unlucky for Mariella, her father took Buster outside to go walkies and found out that it was in fact the middle of the night.

CHAPTER 4

Anti-Matter Rays and Holes in the Fabric of Time

Mariella saw that the Problem of Bedtime No More was far too big for one brain. So the next Monday she asked her science teacher, Mrs Planck, for help.

Mrs Planck understood Mariella's problem.

“Scientists have always wished for more hours in the day,” Mrs Planck said. “And there are only two ways to make this happen. First, you could build an anti-matter ray and blast a hole in the fabric of time itself. Of course, that could destroy the universe. Possibly.”

Mariella didn’t like the idea of destroying the universe. Her dad wouldn’t like it at all.

“And what is the second way?” she asked her teacher.

“You must find a way to travel west at a constant 1,000 miles per hour,” Mrs Planck said. “Then the darkness of night will never catch you.”

‘One thousand miles per hour!’ Mariella thought. ‘That is faster than the fastest bird can fly.’

'But I am not a bird,' she thought as she put one foot on a box. 'I am an inventor!'

CHAPTER 5

Cannons and Catapults (and mashed apple too)

X1000
(?)

Mariella went home and drew her plans on the wallpaper in her bedroom.

She thought about shooting herself out of a cannon, but she didn't want to wake baby Harrison from his nap.

And she thought about a giant catapult, but cutting down all those trees to make one was not very good for the planet.

At last, Mariella decided on a rocket-powered flying suit.

Mariella invented all morning using odds and ends she found around the house or in Dad's shed. It was all stuff she was sure no one would miss.

Hours later, her invention was ready, and Mariella said goodbye to her parents after lunch.

"I am going to orbit the globe at speeds in excess of 1,000 miles per hour," Mariella told Mum.

"Oh, that's lovely, sweetheart," said her mum, who was prodding a spoon of mashed apple at Harrison's head. "Make sure you're home before night falls."

Mariella put her foot up on a handy box. "Trust me, Mum," she said. "I will be EVERYWHERE before night falls."

CHAPTER 6

Spiders and Stars

Lift-off in the rocket-powered flying suit was a total success, but it did cause a five-mile traffic jam in town.

With a little help from a flock of passing geese, Mariella built up enough speed to escape the night. Her speedometer, which she had made from a washing machine dial, told Mariella that she was travelling at 1,050 miles per hour. It also told Mariella that she was out of fabric softener.

'The world looks so different from high up,' Mariella thought.

The city looked like a village, and villages looked like toy towns. And toy towns looked like photos of toy towns, and photos of toy towns looked like beetles. And beetles looked like spiders.

Mariella could see the darkness full of stars flowing behind her, but it couldn't catch her up.

"Bedtime! No more!" she shouted at the top of her voice.

Higher and higher Mariella flew. Faster and faster.

Sometimes her suit malfunctioned, but she found clever ways to fix it.

Sometimes she needed a nap, but she found clever ways to take forty winks without slowing down too much.

Soon the dark was so far behind her that Mariella didn't need to sleep at all.

This gave her plenty of time to think up clever ideas and sketch them into her notebook. She even had enough spare time to land to take on more fuel or for a snack.

And every time Mariella passed over her house, she dropped off presents from faraway lands.

The darkness couldn't get close to her. Mariella was Queen of the Skies.

Bedtime was a thing of the past.

CHAPTER 7

Three Days and Three Nights

But one day Mariella's flying suit had a VERY serious malfunction.

'No problem,' Mariella thought. 'All I need to do is pick one of the amazing ideas in my head to fix it.'

And so Mariella searched her brain for a solution.

But her brain was totally empty.

Mariella was shocked.

Not a single light bulb went off in her mind. She was out of ideas. In all her nine years this had never happened to Mariella before.

'This is a disaster,' Mariella thought. 'What good is an inventor with no ideas?'

Mariella looked back and saw that the darkness was catching up with her. Soon it would wrap itself around her and she would have to go to sleep!

She flicked through her notebook looking for an answer, but none of her clever drawings and diagrams made any sense.

'I'm beginning to nod off,' Mariella realised. 'I'm too tired to think.'

The darkness grew closer and closer.

Mariella diverted all power to the boosters on her suit, but it wasn't enough. Soon she felt her toes tingle and fall asleep, then her feet.

Her dad had a joke that he often told her.

“I hate it when my feet fall asleep in the day,” he’d say almost every evening. “Because then they stay awake all night! Ha ha!”

Mariella always laughed when Dad made his favourite joke, but she was too sleepy to laugh this time.

The darkness crept over Mariella like a soft blanket. And it was so quiet and comfy in there that all of a sudden a snooze seemed like the best idea in the world.

Mariella activated her automatic gliding gear and stretched herself out on a little fluffy cloud, where she slept for three days and three nights.

CHAPTER 8

Jumping Jacks and Snakeskins

When Mariella woke from her sleep on the cloud, she felt different.

'No, I don't feel different,' she thought. 'I feel just the same as I used to.'

Mariella's head was bursting with ideas again.

“What is going on here?” she asked an albatross as it flew past. “Where did all these ideas come from?”

“Awk,” said the albatross, and it flapped away on its huge wings.

“Awk is not the right answer,” Mariella said.

So, after a think, Mariella solved this problem. She used a kind of science sentence called an equation.

The equation went like this –

T = Time

EH = Empty Head

FH = Full Head

Which meant that –

T – 72 hours = EH

T+ ? = FH

So, what was ?

There was only one possible answer.

? = Sleep

Mariella was a super smart person, and so she soon worked out that while she'd been asleep her brain had recharged.

More sleep meant better ideas.

Time + Sleep = Full Head

“Aha!” Mariella said. “Now I’ve worked it out. Sleep makes you smarter.”

Mariella did 25 jumping jacks to get her blood pumping nice and fast, then she used her fresh ideas to fix the flying suit.

It was so easy!

Mariella used an old snakeskin to patch her wing, and then she used the heat from an erupting volcano to make the patch stick.

Mariella couldn't believe that she hadn't thought of this before.

CHAPTER 9

New Friends and Lollipops

Mariella made one last orbit of the Earth, but this time she took it nice and slow.

Mariella realised that things look much more beautiful when you don't zoom past them at 1,000 miles per hour.

Mariella slept when she was tired, and she even landed a few times to make new friends and take some selfies.

At last, Mariella arrived home to a hero's welcome.

Her baby brother Harrison's weight had increased by 4% and his hugs were now 10% tighter.

That night, Mariella was writing up her report when Harrison toddled upstairs to ask her if she could invent an everlasting lollipop.

Mariella put her foot on a box and said, "Let me sleep on it."

And she did.

Our books are tested
for children and young people by
children and young people.

Thanks to everyone who consulted on
a manuscript for their time and effort in
helping us to make our books better
for our readers.